MAC THE MAGNIFICENT MOUSE

Follows Directions

Written by: **Ann B. Rhodes**   Illustrator: **Nolan Moore**

WIN 2 PUBLISHING, LLC

Dedication

This book is dedicated to my mom, Alma Rhodes, who has always supported me in everything that I have done, my 2 brothers, Bennie, Jr. and Roy Lee, my niece, Tianna Rhodes, and all of the students that I have taught throughout the years.

Mac the Magnificent mouse

MAC
City
School

visits different schools throughout the **land.**

Elementary
School
Store
MAC

He hides in classroom corners
to see which students raise their **hand.**

What is a noun?
noun: a person, place, or thing.
ex: car, computer, truck, store, teacher, daughter, lawyer.
1 2 3 4 5 6 7 8 9 10
Aa Bb Cc Dd Ee Ff Gg Hh Ii Jj
Yy Zz

He looks for who completes their work,
and who stays in their **seat.**

These are the very students who
know how to stay off their **feet.**

9 10
Nn Oo Pp Qq Rr Ss
Gg Hh Ii Jj Kk Ll Mm
Tt Uu Vv Ww Xx Yy Zz
Aa Bb Cc Dd Ee Ff

Some students were reading books
while others were working **alone.**

Mac the Magnificent mouse checked
that no one was on the **phone.**

English
and
Grammar

Every student's materials were arranged neatly
while each desk was six feet **apart.**

Even though things were a little bit different
these kids did great, they were **smart!**

Students are in their classroom at lunchtime while teachers created brain **breaks.**

Instruction consisted of hands-on learning where there were lots of neat things they could **make.**

Mac the Magnificent mouse
wanted to make sure everyone washed their **hands.**

That they know how to follow class rules
and each student knew where to **stand.**

EXIT
BOYS
GIRLS
6ft. apart
6ft. apart

For any students who were lost on directions,
Mac the Magnificent mouse helped them find their
listening **ear**.

He wanted to make sure that all of the boys and girls
knew exactly what to **hear**.

Math
1×7 = 7
2×7 = 14
3×7 = 21
4×7 = 2

As Mac the Magnificent mouse left the school
there was an idea that came to **mind.**

Treat everyone with love, respect, and obedience.
And to everyone, always be **kind.**

These students showed obedience and were Kind to each other.

Mac the Magnificent Mouse
Follows Directions

Mac the Magnificent mouse is a mouse that goes around to visit boys and girls at school, but he is there to see who is not doing the right thing. No one can see Mac the Mouse because he is always in a corner watching, but one day he appears to offer some guidance of help. This book is the first in the children' book series: Mac the Magnificent mouse to teach students how to show positive behavior.

Acknowledgements

I would like to give a special thank you for my amazing illustrator, Nolan Moore. He did an outstanding job with the illustrations. I also want to give a special shout out to my wonderful mentor, Ellaine Ursuy. She was able guide me through this process.

About the Author

Ann Rhodes is a self-published author from Georgia. She started writing when she was 8 years old. She has always enjoyed writing poetry. Her poems were published in the school and local newspapers. Since 2016, she has published 2 poetry books and 2 devotional books.

Mac the Magnificent mouse is her first children's book. She was inspired to write a children's book from her background of being an elementary school teacher. When she was placed in 2nd grade and had to teach reading every day, her number one goal was to write a children's book.

About the Illustrator

Nolan Moore is an illustrator from Grand Rapids, Michigan. He graduated from the University of Michigan-Flint in 2017 with a bachelor's in business management. He loves koalas, sports, and drawing. He is very thankful for the ways that his family and friends encouraged him to pursue art and illustrating. You can follow him on Facebook and Instagram at Nolan Moore Illustrations or email him at **Nolan.moore.illustrations@gmail.com**.

If you have enjoyed this children's book by Ann B. Rhodes, please feel free to check out her other books on Amazon:

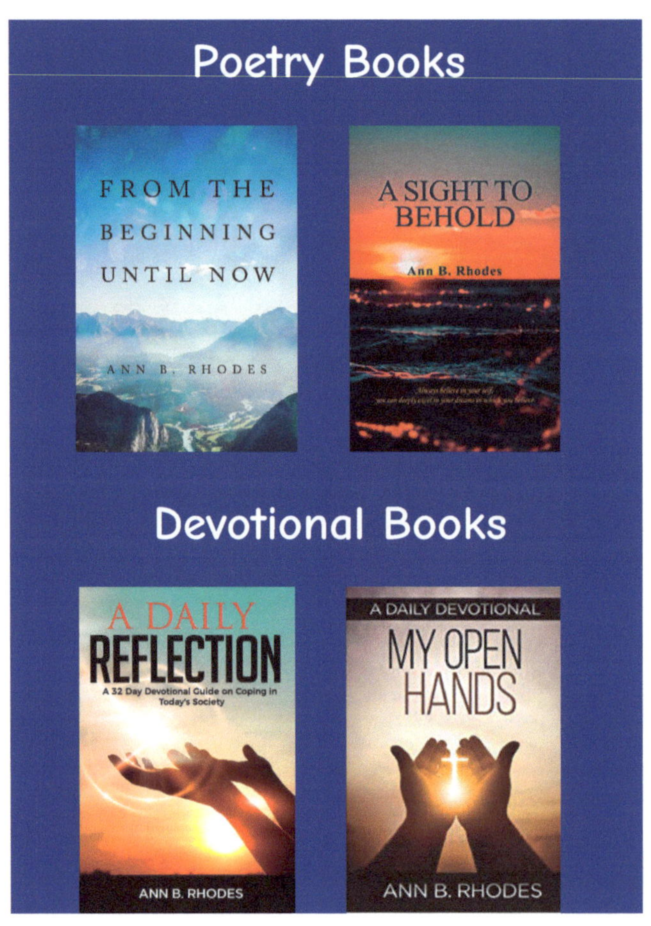

What did I learn the most?

Mac the Magnificent mouse helped me

____

____

It is important to raise your hand because

____

____

Why is it important to stay in your seat while you work?

____

____

Which school rule do you have a difficult time following?

____

____

What did you like the most about Mac the Magnificent mouse?

____

____

*Remember if you enjoyed this book, please write a review.

Draw a picture of the next adventure for Mac the Magnificent Mouse.

9 781733 322256